Backstage
at the School Play

by Alison Reynolds

illustrated by Dylan Gibson

raintree

a Capstone company — publishers for children

Engage Literacy is published in the UK by Raintree.
Raintree is an imprint of Capstone Global Library Limited, a company incorporated
in England and Wales having its registered office at 264 Banbury Road, Oxford,
OX2 7DY – Registered company number: 6695582

www.raintree.co.uk

Printed and bound in India.

Backstage at the School Play

ISBN: 978 1 4747 1820 2

Contents

Chapter 1
The perfect play 4

Chapter 2
Thunder and lightning 8

Chapter 3
Lights out! 12

Chapter 4
A fright in the dark 16

Chapter 5
Sound and light effects 20

Chapter 6
Coloured lights 24

Chapter 7
The show must go on 26

Chapter 8
A big success 30

Chapter 1

The perfect play

Raj leaped onto the stage. In exactly four hours and fifty-one seconds the play would start. He looked over his list. Being director, writer and main actor was a big responsibility, but he knew he could do it.

Mr Bracks, Raj's teacher, stood at the door. "You look organised, Raj. I'm in the school office if you need me."

Raj nodded, studying his list. "Caitlin, are the costumes ready?"

"Yes." Her arms were full of costumes.

"Jez and Ari, are the sets in place?"

"Yes," said Jez. "We're just waiting for Mia to check that the lights are in the right places."

"Where is Mia?" Raj frowned.

Just then the door creaked open, and Mia crept in.

"Glad you're here," said Raj. "All ready?"

Mia's cheeks turned red as she walked to the stage, staring at her feet.

"Let's go," said Raj.

Mia tripped as she walked up the stage stairs.

Raj pointed to the table at the side of the stage. "You can set up over there."

The chair scraped across the shiny, wooden floorboards as Mia sat down.

She opened her laptop.

"OK?" asked Jez.

She nodded. "The sound and lights for the show should all work."

"It must be perfect," said Raj. "*Camp Wrong* is going to be the best play our school has ever seen."

Mia gulped.

"You're a whizz, Mia," said Jez.

Ari nodded. "It's amazing how you can run all the sounds and lights from your laptop."

Jez whispered, "Don't worry about Raj. He just wants the play to be perfect."

Mia smiled. The sound and light computer program was all she had been working on for weeks. This was her big chance to show the school what she could do, even if she was shy and didn't talk much.

"I'll do a last run-through," she said.

Chapter 2

Thunder and lightning

"Are the lights ready?" asked Raj nervously. "It's show time in one hour."

"Nearly," said Mia. "Check that spotlight, Ari."

"Sure. How does this one bright light change into so many colours?"

"With my laptop I can move coloured sheets in front of the white light, making different coloured beams. A beam is the glowing light that shines straight out ahead."

"As long as it works," said Raj. "OK, let's ..." He stopped. A flash of lightning lit up the room. "Quick, close the blinds!"

Raj ran towards the windows. "Help!" he yelled. A clap of thunder shook the building.

Mia, Jez and Ari looked at each other, wondering what was wrong with Raj. Ari shrugged and ran to close the rest of the blinds.

"How great would it be if there was a real live thunderstorm during the play, Mia?" asked Ari. "We wouldn't need your special effects."

"One cat and dog, two cat and dog, three cat and dog..." counted Jez. "The thunderstorm's going away, so we will need you after all, Mia."

She grinned. "After all this work, that's good."

"What's with the cat and dogs?" asked Ari.

"You can tell how far away a storm is by counting between the lightning flash and the thunder," said Jez. "Each five seconds is one mile. I counted up to fifteen seconds, so it's three miles away now."

Ari looked around. "Where's Raj?"

"In here." Raj's voice sounded far away.

Jez tiptoed up to the small door under the stage and knocked. "Raj?"

The door swung open. "Now that the storm's over, back to work."

"Why were you in there?" asked Ari.

"Just checking." Mia, Ari and Jez glanced at each other.

Outside there was the sound of cars arriving.

"Come on," ordered Raj. "Everyone is here."

"That was weird," said Jez.

Mia nodded. Something was really odd.

Chapter 3

Lights out!

The room filled with children and teachers.

"Can I have sound?" asked Raj.

Mia nodded and clicked her computer mouse.

A screech rang out, making everybody cover their ears with their hands.

"Sorry, feedback. Move the speakers forward, please. The microphone is picking up sound from them, causing the noise."

Raj started again. "You all know what to do, *Camp Wrong* will be perfect. We can do this, people." Raj pumped his arm in the air.

Everybody cheered.

Lightning flashed around the edges of the blinds. A crash of thunder boomed and the room went dark.

"Agghh!" Raj grabbed onto Mia's arm.

"No cat and dogs between that lightning and thunder," said Ari.

"Yeah," said Jez, "the storm is right over us."

More lightning flashed and thunder boomed.

Suddenly, there was silence.

Raj let go of Mia's arm. "Can somebody turn on the lights?"

There was a clicking sound. "I'm trying," said Jez. "The electricity's out."

"No show tonight," said Raj. "Everybody, call your parents to get you."

"We have to do the play," said Mia.

"It's dangerous," said Raj. "There might be another thunderstorm."

"We're safe in here because lightning's only dangerous when you're outside. Thunder can't hurt you. It's only a noise."

"I'm sure the teachers agree with me that we shouldn't have the show tonight."

Raj's voice sounded hopeful as he spoke to the dark room.

Mr Bracks answered, "Maybe, although we like to encourage our students to be..."

Mia stood up tall. "We can do this."

"Our parents can bring torches or the lights off our bikes," suggested Jez.

"We can use musical instruments to make sound effects," said Mia.

Raj said slowly, "But the lightning."

"You're safe in here," said Mr Bracks.

"The show must go on," said Mia.

Everyone started clapping and cheering.

Chapter 4

A fright in the dark

"I'll find some instruments." Mia tried not to think how lonely and scary it would be walking to the music room alone.

"I'll bring my bike light," offered Raj.

"Thanks." Suddenly, Mia felt much better.

Flicking on his bike light, Raj said, "Follow me."

As they walked through the shadowy school building, Mia shivered. Although she understood shadows were just places that the light couldn't reach, it still seemed spooky.

Raj stopped outside the music room.

"Why's the door open?" asked Mia. "It's always kept shut."

They stared at the door, lit only by the bike light, watching it slowly open.

Creak.

Mia and Raj moved closer together and stepped inside.

There was a swish, swish noise.

"What's that?" whispered Raj.

The door slammed shut behind them, making Mia's heart thump.

The bike light flickered in Raj's shaking hand. "Do you think we should leave?"

Bang!

"Ahhhh!" yelled Mia and Raj, jumping in the air.

"Spooked you," shouted two voices.

Raj pointed his bike light in the direction of the voices. "Jez? Ari?"

Ari laughed. "Scared by the big bass drum and brushes on the snare drum."

Jez looked at Mia. "Sorry."

"Then why do it?" Mia's voice sounded angry.

"We'll do the sound effects to make up for it, Mia," said Jez. "Just tell us what to do."

The four picked up as many instruments as they could carry.

"Maybe, the show will go on," said Raj. He led the way with his bike light.

Chapter 5
Sound and light effects

A spotlight lit up the stage.

"It runs on a battery, but hopefully it will last the show," said Mr Bracks.

Raj banged the drumstick on the bass drum. A noise boomed as the drum skin vibrated, or moved back and forth quickly. "Thunder is ready."

"And we can use the brushes to make the swishing sound of the windscreen wipers on the bus."

Ari blew into a trumpet. "Bus horn."

Jez tucked a violin under his chin. "I'll provide the music if anybody wants to help," he suggested.

There was a chorus of yes.

"OK," said Raj. "The bus bringing the children to camp drives along in the rain."

Jez played the snare drum softly with different brushes.

"There's a thunderstorm." Raj banged the bass drum. "A rabbit bounces across the road and the driver honks his horn."

Ari gave a blast on the trumpet.

"The bus brakes."

Jez screeched the violin.

"And drives into a ditch."

A saxophone made a loud, low sound.

Raj clapped. "This could work, guys. We just need the lighting."

"I'm working on it." Mia waved to a pile of torches by her feet.

"But how will the campfire look real as the children wait to be rescued?" Raj frowned.

"I have an idea," Mia said excitedly. She pointed to a stack of rear red bike reflectors. "The small plastic rectangles shine when light hits them."

"Will that work?" Raj asked in a worried voice.

"You wait until I shine a light on the reflectors, and the light bounces off. It will make a red glow."

"Excellent." Raj grinned. "I'll change into my bus driver costume before people arrive, but remember..."

Mia, Jez and Ari said all together, "Everything has to be perfect!"

Chapter 6
Coloured lights

Mia clapped her hands over her mouth. "I forgot that we don't have coloured sheets for the torches. So how can we have different colours of light?"

"Does it matter?" asked Ari.

"Yes," snapped Mia. "I want blue lighting for the spooky scene when the children gather around the campfire. I also wanted yellow lighting to show their joy when they're rescued. I would've switched on the red and green sheets to get a yellow glow."

Jez scratched his head. "What do the coloured sheets do exactly?"

"They split light beams into different colours," said Mia. "The whole play will be wrecked without them."

"What about thin plastic?" suggested Ari. "We could find different colours. It would need to be transparent, so light can shine through. We could hold the plastic over our lights, changing the colour of the beams."

"Maybe." Mia thought hard. "If we put green plastic over red plastic."

"Come on, Ari," said Jez. "Let's look in the art room."

Mia bit her lip. If the lighting didn't work, the play would be a flop, and it would be all her fault. She was the one who said the show must go on.

Chapter 7
The show must go on

Mia studied the crowd. Even though she couldn't really see them in the dim light, she could hear them. Everybody was waiting for *Camp Wrong* to begin.

The campers gathered in pairs. They formed a line behind Raj, who stood at the front with a steering wheel.

"Off we go to Camp Rightside," called Raj.

Ari and Jez crept up in the shadows, shining torches in front of Raj. It looked just like two headlights shining out.

"Rain," whispered Mia.

Jez gently brushed the snare drum, which sounded exactly like rain.

Mia let out a slow breath. Perhaps everything would be OK.

"Thunderstorm," she said.

Jez banged the bass drum.

"Lightning first," hissed Mia.

"Sorry." Jez held the drumstick in the air.

Ari flashed a light, then Jez slammed down the drumsticks.

Another crash followed, but it was outside, where a real thunderstorm was starting. Flashes of light lit up the room. Then there was a clap of thunder, which was so loud it made everybody jump.

Raj zoomed past Mia's table in the wing.

"Where are you going?" Mia chased him off the stage, and down the back stairs. She shone her torch on him. "Stop."

Raj turned around, blinking in the light.

"What's going on, Raj?" she asked in a soft voice.

"The thunderstorm."

"You're not frightened." Mia waited. "Are you?"

Raj nodded. "We have to stop the play."

"But lightning's just a bolt of electricity in the sky, and we are safe while we are inside. Thunder..."

"It's too scary," Raj said slowly.

"That's ..." Mia stopped herself from saying "That's silly." That's what people always said to her when she was too shy to speak. "You know how you struck the bass drum before?"

"Yes."

"That's like thunder. It's just the sound of air moving caused by a lightning bolt, instead of by a drumstick."

Raj was silent. If he thought about thunder that way, it didn't seem so scary.

"Let's go back?" Mia started up the stairs.

Raj smiled. "We've got a show."

Chapter 8

A big success

Raj bounced back onto stage. "A short break." He grinned at Mia, who smiled back from the stage wing.

The thunderstorm raged outside, but the thunderstorm inside was even bigger. The bass drum crashed, and the torches flickered.

"Oh no, a rabbit," shouted Raj.

Then, Raj swerved, skidded on the wet road, and drove into a ditch. The campers screamed, and the people watching gasped.

The thunderstorms both inside and outside came to an end. The campers decided to build a fire while waiting to be rescued.

Ari waved a small light towards the pretend fire. The crowd laughed when they saw the stack of red bike reflectors. But it really did look a little bit like a flickering campfire.

Jez held a piece of blue plastic in front of Mia's white spotlight. It created a spooky glow as the campers told ghost stories.

The play was a big success.

The crowd cheered for the performers.

Raj bowed and looked around him. "I couldn't have done it without all of you. It was a team effort."

"Let's do every play without electricity," said Jez.

"Mia saved the day!" said Raj, turning to look at her.

Even though her legs felt shaky, Mia left the safety of the wing and walked across the stage.

She bowed and cleared her throat.
"It was a perfect play, Raj."

Everybody clapped and cheered.